HANA, THE NO-COW WIFE

To Sarah, Jordan, and Anna—PB

To Zachary—WT

Suggested by the original story "Johnny Lingo and the Eight-cow Wife,"
copyright © 1965 by Patricia McGerr, first published in *Woman's Day*.

© 1993 Deseret Book Company

Deseret Book is a registered trademark of Deseret Book Company.

Printed in Hong Kong.

10 9 8 7 6 5 4 3 2 1

ISBN 0-87579-714-8

Designed by Richard Erickson and Pat Bagley.
Illustrations were done with acrylics on textured board.
Text was set in Baskerville.

HANA, THE
NO-COW WIFE

WRITTEN BY PAT BAGLEY · ILLUSTRATED BY WILL TERRY

DESERET BOOK COMPANY
AND PRIMARY PRESS
SALT LAKE CITY, UTAH

In the islands they tell the story of Johnny Lingo and how he married the shy Mahana. As was customary, he offered cows to her parents as tokens of his love. Two or three cows were about as much honor as any girl could expect, but Johnny surprised everyone. He gave an excessive number of cows—eight, to be exact—for Mahana.

The other girls were upset—why would the handsome Johnny Lingo marry someone so plain? They just couldn't understand it.

Encouraged by her newfound standing as an eight-cow wife, Mahana began to feel and act and look like a real catch. In truth, she and Johnny made quite a handsome couple.

Their story became a big hit.

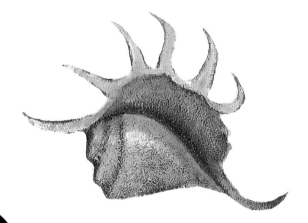

Parents in nearby villages loved telling the story of Johnny and Mahana almost as much as their children loved hearing it.

One girl in particular couldn't get enough of the tale—especially the part about the eight cows. Her name was Hana, and she would pester her parents until one of them finally gave in and told the story for the millionth time.

These repeated tellings had a strange effect on the girl: she began to confuse cows with love. The more cows, she thought, the deeper the love. So by the time Hana was old enough to think about marriage, she resolved she wouldn't go for fewer than nine cows.

She could have gotten them too.

Hana was beautiful. Her lips were as red as coral, and her eyes, as lustrous as black pearls. So what if she spent too much time gazing into her mother's mirror or leafing through glamour magazines? Her many handsome boyfriends didn't seem to mind. They would hang out in designer lava-lavas and compete to offer her rides in their hot outriggers equipped with state-of-the-art sound systems.

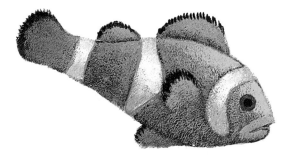

Meanwhile, on the far side of the island lived a young man named Kona. He was poor, and his sole possession was a rather shabby cow. To Kona, however, his cow wasn't shabby at all—he considered her the most beautiful cow alive.

Kona was like that. The splendor of the simplest flower dazzled him. A common finch fascinated him more than the biggest outrigger on the island.

Living things responded to Kona's attention. Plants grew lushly by his shack, and birds outdid themselves creating songs to delight him. Animals chittered happily behind him when he walked through the jungle.

The islanders thought him a trifle odd.

One day as Kona strolled through the island, he heard laughter so melodious that the birds stopped singing and cocked their heads to listen. Through the trees, he caught a glimpse of Hana sitting beside the ocean.

The poor boy didn't stand a chance. Before Hana had wandered out of sight, Kona was in love.

But his heart sank. To win Hana's love, he must follow the island custom and give away his cow. How could he part with such a treasured friend?

For days Kona was torn between his faithful cow and his memory of the beautiful Hana. Finally, he decided.

"Cow," he spoke softly into the animal's ear, "will you give yourself so I do not go empty-handed to the beautiful Hana? Surely she will see you are the best of cows and not turn me away." Kona looked into the cow's eyes as she gravely nodded her consent.

The next day Kona visited Hana and spoke his heart. Hana sized up his tattered clothes and pitiful cow and snickered. "You must be joking. I'd be laughed at even to be seen with you! And as for that bag of bones you call a cow, a dozen more just like her wouldn't come close to my true worth!" Then she turned away and went inside to watch TV.

Heartbroken, Kona sadly led his beloved cow away.

That night, Hana dreamed a dream. She stood on the beach, encircled by an assembly of cows. In the light of a bonfire, she saw them turn their solemn eyes toward her.

Hana blinked. "Of course!" she thought, "I'm worth all these handsome cows, and they are here to honor me." She silently began to count them. Hana could just imagine what people would say of her . . . twelve? . . . fifteen? . . . twenty?—

One, larger than the rest, interrupted her counting. "Look at yourself."

Hana was surprised to find that she held her mother's mirror. She raised it and looked. Gazing back at her was a repulsive creature. The thing's lips were smeared red, and its eyes were caked shut with mascara. She was horrified when the monster smugly said, "A dozen more just like you wouldn't come close to my true worth." Hana dropped the mirror.

She heard the cows talking among themselves. "This is the girl who smothers joy when she speaks," said one. "This is the girl who has eyes only for her own beauty," said another. The chief cow's eyes blazed as she raised an accusing hoof at Hana. "This is the girl who is not worth one of us!"

Cows with flared nostrils pawed the ground. Hana gasped fearfully as she imagined herself trampled under angry hooves.

"Wait!" came a voice. The crowd grew still as Kona's cow stepped forward. Hana remembered how she had cruelly insulted this animal. Shame joined her fear, both eating at her like hungry sharks. Surely Kona's cow had come to condemn her.

"I cannot dispute your judgment of this girl," began the cow. "She is indeed vain, and her heart is cold. But you know my master and how he loves us. He also loves this girl and sees good in her. For his sake I ask that you delay judgment."

"Very well," said the chief. "We shall wait to see if she has some good in her . . ."

Hana awoke with a start. Outside her window, waiting patiently in the moonlight, stood Kona's cow. Hana knew what she must do. She quickly dressed and followed the cow into the night.

By sunrise she stood uncertainly at Kona's door. Naturally, Kona was surprised to see her. But he didn't forget his manners—he offered her a place to sit and something to drink.

For one so out of practice, Hana did an admirable job of apologizing. As she left, she again caught sight of the cow. This time she looked with wonder: never had she seen such loving eyes.

Hana returned to visit Kona. Her visits, rare at first, became more frequent as she saw that Kona wasn't the simpleton she'd imagined.

She could not resist his love of living things. She enjoyed the riot of birds and beasts that attended him. She learned the language of animals. The birds taught her their songs. Her laughter, which was a wonder to begin with, grew even richer. She came to see all creatures as precious.

Curiously, the more time she spent with Kona, the more shallow and boring her old boyfriends seemed.

In time, Hana and Kona married. Hana caused a stir by refusing to allow Kona to give his cow to her parents. She playfully said that such a beautiful animal was easily worth eight wives. The island boys were upset that the beautiful Hana would marry that peculiar fellow from across the island. They just couldn't understand it.

In the islands they still talk of her: Hana, the no-cow wife.